Five Little Ducks

Distributed by The Child's World®
1980 Lookout Drive • Mankato, MN 56003-1705
800-599-READ • www.childsworld.com

Acknowledgments
The Child's World®: Mary Berendes, Publishing Director
The Design Lab: Kathleen Petelinsek, Design and Page Production

Library of Congress Cataloging-in-Publication Data
Weidner, Teri.
  Five little ducks / illustrated by Teri Weidner.
    p. cm.
  Summary: A duck with a feather on his back leads his siblings with a
"quack, quack, quack." End notes list the benefits of nursery rhymes.
  ISBN 978-1-60253-528-2 (library bound : alk. paper)
  1. Nursery rhymes. 2. Children's poetry. [1. Nursery rhymes.] I. Title.
  PZ8.3.W417Fi 2010
  398.8—dc22   2010015199

Printed in the United States of America in Mankato, Minnesota.
July 2010
F11538

DEC 2011 ILLUSTRATED BY TERI WEIDNER

Five little ducks that I once knew . . .
fat ones, skinny ones, tall ones, too.

But the one little duck
with the feather on his back,
he ruled the others with a
quack, quack, quack!

Quack, quack, quack!
Quack, quack, quack!
He ruled the others with a
quack, quack, quack!

Down to the river they would go,
wibble, wobble, wibble, wobble,
all in a row.

But the one little duck
with the feather on his back,
he ruled the others with a
quack, quack, quack!

Quack, quack, quack!
Quack, quack, quack!

He ruled the others with a
quack, quack, quack!

POEM ACTIVITY

Five little ducks that I once knew . . .
>**Hold up five fingers.**

fat ones, skinny ones, tall ones, too.
>**Move your hands wide apart, close together, and then high above your head.**

But the one little duck with the feather on his back,
he ruled the others with a *quack, quack, quack!*
>**Put one hand on your back like a feather and wave it.**

Quack, quack, quack! Quack, quack, quack!
He ruled the others with a *quack, quack, quack!*
>**Make a duck's-bill shape with your hands in front of your mouth. Open and close it when you quack!**

Down to the river they would go,
wibble, wobble, wibble, wobble, all in a row.
>**Wobble back and forth.**

But the one little duck with the feather on his back,
he ruled the others with a *quack, quack, quack!*
>**Put one hand on your back like a feather and wave it.**

Quack, quack, quack! Quack, quack, quack!
He ruled the others with a *quack, quack, quack!*
>**Make a duck's-bill shape with your hands in front of your mouth. Open and close it when you quack!**

BENEFITS OF CHILDREN'S POEMS AND SONGS

Children's poems and songs are more than just a fun way to pass the time. They are a rich source of intellectual, emotional, and physical development for a young child. Here are some of their benefits:

* Learning the words and activities builds the child's self-confidence—"I can do it all by myself!"

* The repetitious movements build coordination and motor skills.

* The close physical interaction between adult and child reinforces both physical and emotional bonding.

* In a context of "fun," the child learns the art of listening in order to learn.

* Learning the words expands the child's vocabulary. He or she learns the names of objects and actions that are both familiar and new.

* Repeating the words helps develop the child's memory.

* Learning the words is an important step toward learning to read.

* Reciting the words gives the child a grasp of English grammar and how it works. This enhances the development of language skills.

* The rhythms and rhyming patterns sharpen listening skills and teach the child how poetry works. Eventually the child learns to put together his or her own simple rhyming words—"I made a poem!"

ABOUT THE ILLUSTRATOR

Teri Weidner grew up in Fairport, New York, where she spent much of her free time drawing horses and other animals. Today, she is delighted to have a career illustrating books for children. She lives in Portsmouth, New Hampshire with her husband and a menagerie of pets.

JESUS LOVES ME

Little Shepherd
an imprint of Scholastic Inc.
New York

Jesus loves me! This I know,

For the Bible tells me so.

They are weak, but He is strong

Yes, Jesus loves me!
Yes, Jesus loves me!

Jesus loves me! He who died,

Heaven's gate to open wide.

He will wash away my sin;

Yes, Jesus loves me!
Yes, Jesus loves me!

The Bible
tells me so.